Adapted by
Victoria Saxon

Illustrated by
Vivien Wu

Designed by
Tony Fejeran

🌸 A GOLDEN BOOK • NEW YORK

Lightning McQueen was the best racer in the Piston Cup. He was *quicker* than *quick*, *faster* than *fast*. He was **speed**!

Long ago, Lightning had the best coach in the world. His name was **Doc Hudson**.

Doc taught Lightning to **work hard** and to *love racing*.

Now Lightning was competing against a new racer named **Jackson Storm**. He was from the next generation of race cars.

Lightning raced as fast and as hard as he could . . .

. . . but he *lost control* . . .

. . . and *crashed*!

Lightning would not give up! Four months later, he was determined to compete in the new racing season.

To prepare for the first race in Florida, he went to a high-tech training facility.

"Welcome!" said Lightning's new sponsor, Sterling. "I'm your biggest fan."

Soon Lightning met a young trainer named **Cruz Ramirez**. She was the best trainer around.

Cruz made Lightning do strange exercises. "We need to loosen those ancient joints!" she said. Lightning wanted to try a fancy racing simulator, but Cruz thought he wasn't ready. He tried it anyway . . .

. . . and he ***broke*** it!

Lightning had one last chance to prove he could still compete. He went to a local beach to get his tires dirty with some real training.

Cruz went with Lightning to help him, but she had **never raced outside**. Perhaps the beach wasn't the best place to train. . . .

Lightning wanted to compete in a real race. He and Cruz went to **Thunder Hollow Speedway** and wore disguises so no one would recognize them. They soon discovered the race was a **demolition derby**!

Lightning tried his best. He *dodged* and *weaved* to avoid other cars.

He helped Cruz when the fierce school bus
Miss Fritter charged at her. Then Cruz accidentally
knocked over a water truck, which *sprayed away*
Lightning's disguise. The crowd was shocked to see
Lightning McQueen!

After the race, Lightning was upset. The training wasn't working. He was taking care of Cruz instead of focusing on racing. Then Lightning discovered that Cruz had wanted to race all her life. She'd lost her confidence, though. She became a trainer instead.

Lightning had an idea. He and Cruz went to Doc Hudson's hometown: **Thomasville**. They took a spin around the track.

Then they saw a figure in the distance.
His name was **Smokey**. He had coached
Doc in his racing days!

Smokey took Lightning and Cruz to meet the Legends, a group of Doc's racing friends from the old days. They had been waiting a long time to meet Doc's former student.

The Legends had lots of stories to share. They even told Lightning and Cruz about Doc's amazing *flip*. Doc hadn't been the fastest racer, but he had been the smartest.

Smokey agreed to coach Lightning, and
Cruz became Lightning's training partner. They
worked on their speed and agility by weaving
through a herd of tractors.

Lightning worked hard. Before the big competition in Florida, he raced Cruz one last time around the Thomasville track. He gave it everything he had, but before he knew it—

ZOOOOM!

Cruz won!

Now it was time to go to Florida. When Lightning arrived, he was nervous. He didn't know if he could win. If this was the end of his career, he would be heartbroken, like Doc had been.

Smokey said that Doc had loved racing, but he'd loved being Lightning's crew chief even more.

"He saw something in you that you don't even see in yourself," Smokey told Lightning.

The race was about to begin. But Lightning thought about Cruz. She had trained with him—and had even beaten him in a race! He knew she should be living her dream as a racer. She just needed a chance.

Suddenly, Lightning had an *idea*.

He would leave the race, and Cruz would finish it! Lightning believed in her, just like Doc had believed in him. Ramone gave her a cool new paint job with the *number 95*!

Cruz was nervous at first, but Lightning **supported** her from the crew chief stand. She quickly sped past the other racers.

When Cruz caught up to Jackson Storm, he pushed her into the wall. But Cruz remembered Doc's amazing trick—and she flipped over Storm! **_Cruz won the race!_**

Cruz's racing career was just beginning, and Lightning's career at the track was far from finished. Together they made an **unstoppable team**.